Rellf

the Baker Elf

A Story of Friendship and Following Your Dreams

by
Rick Kwedder

Snow is falling on the village of the Baker Elves.

There lives a little elf named Rellf, with his sister, mother and father. The Baker Elves have an important job of baking the cookies for the gift making elves. Rellf is beginning baking school soon.

Rellf's dream is to be a letter reading elf, but Rellf has a little bit of a problem, he doesn't read very well.

Letter reading elves need to be very, very good at reading. They read about ten letters, per hour, each day!

Rellf's mother told him what the letter reading elves do every day.

Rellf asked his Momma, "Do you think that I will ever be really good at reading? And quick too? Just like I am with baking?"

Momma replied, "Rellf you bake a little different from all the other Baker Elves, because you look at the pictures instead of reading the directions. Son your cookies and cakes are some of the best in the village, even though you have a hard time reading. So, if your dream is to be a letter reading elf then I cannot think of an elf better for the job."

Rellf became more and more scared, as the days crept closer, for him to start baking school. Because student elves have to read the directions out-loud as part of their school work to be a baker elf.

Snow glistened on the first day of baking school.
All the little elves ran to the school because they
could not wait to get inside.

Baking School

Rellf sat outside with his parents.

His dad patted him on the back and said, "Don't be so apprehensive to go in."

Rellf turned around and asked his dad, "What does apprehensive mean?"

He told him, "It means to be scared or worried about doing something."

Then Relif's mom knelt down next to him, while looking at the glistening snow. She picked some of it up and said, "Each elf shines in different parts of life, just like this snow. With work you can shine in many parts of life."

She smiled at him and they walked inside.

Rellf stepped into the snow globe classroom.

Ms. Snowcap said, "it's nice to meet you Rellf, please take a seat."

Rellf mumbled, "It's nice to meet you too" and then he sat down at his desk.

The little elf sitting next to him was in a little red sled.

Rellf asked the little elf, "What's your name?"

The little elf said joyfully, "My name is Ed."

Rellf looked at him curiously and said, "Ed, why are you in that sled?"

Ed replied, "What is your name friend?"

Rellf quietly answered, "I am Rellf."

Ed smiled and said, "Well Rellf, I cannot walk so Santa built this sled for me."

A friendship was made that day.

Weeks after the first day of school, Rellf was crying in his room because he was struggling to read the letters. Letters were flipping around in his head when he read the word chocolate over and over again. He was so mad at himself. Rellf could not understand why all the elves could read so much better than him. He wanted to give up because at school tomorrow there is a reading test, the first one. Rellf's mom knocked at his door. She opened it slowly, she shut it behind her.

She said, "Rellf I have news to tell you. Ed has to have surgery on his legs and hands, so they can move a little bit better."

After that, Rellf realized he couldn't give up on his dream of becoming a letter reading elf, just like Ed would not give up on his dream of building Santa a new sled.

Rellf came down from his room to eat dinner and sat down at the table. The plate of food that Rellf's mom put on the table made his homework drop to the floor.

Rellf's sister picked it up and asked him, "Would you like your big sisters help with this homework when we are done?"

Rellf replied, "Yes, please" as she handed it back to him.

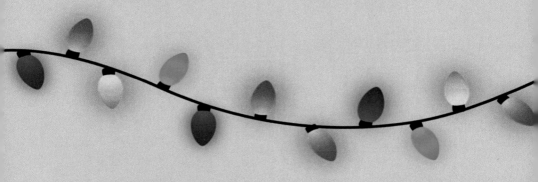

After dinner, Rellf and his sister sat on the couch together.

She read, "The boy was so happy because he made cookies by himself. Rellf can you read that sentence back to me?"

Rellf replied, "I will try, but what if I can't do it?"

His sister gently smiled and said, "Mom, dad and I will still be proud of you for trying!"

Rellf smiled because he knew he could do anything with the love of his family.

"The test is today!" Ms. Snowcap said.

She explained that there are three different tests if you want to do something else in the village. Rellf was getting a little sick to his tummy, at his desk, because he was nervous. A little elf passed the first test back to Rellf. At that point, Rellf started crying and began thinking he couldn't follow his dream.

He must have said it out loud, because Ms. Snowcap came over and told him, "It's the baking test, you've got this one."

Rellf passed that test in five minutes. It took him five years to finish the other two, but he did it.

Today, Rellf is the top letter reading elf in the workshop.

Postscript:

The sled that Ed wanted to build for Santa was made a few weeks after he got out of the hospital. Ed had a little help in making Santa's red sled. Relif built half of it by the time Ed got home. Ed was very happy when he saw the half built sled.

He said, "Relif why did you do this for me?"

Relif said, "Because you are my friend and that is what friendship is all about. Helping your friends with their dreams."

Relif and Ed worked for two weeks on the sled and they gave it to Santa on Christmas Eve.

The jolly old man said, "This is the best gift because Christmas is about kindness."

Merry Christmas

Made in the USA
Monee, IL,
24 November 2020

49437609R00021